To Deacon:

Enjoy this

book

Love
Mrs. Wirger
3-20-13

A
GOOD
MORNING'S
WORK

Steck-Vaughn Company
Austin, Texas

A GOOD MORNING'S WORK

by Nathan Zimelman
illustrated by Carol Rogers

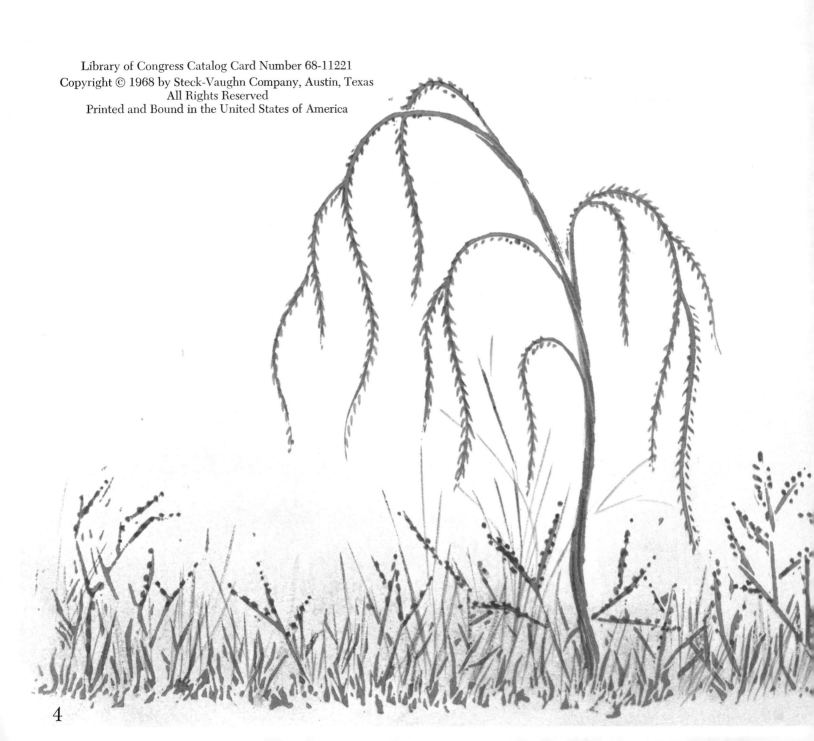

Mitsuo Yamada leaned on his hoe and sighed deeply. "It will be a long, long day," he said to himself.

"Mitsuo! Mitsuo, have you started to clear the weeds?" his father called.

Hurriedly Mitsuo raised the hoe and called out, "I have begun, Father."

Mitsuo looked at the hoe as it sank into the soft brown earth. "I have begun," he said to himself. Pulling as hard as he could, he cut a long brown furrow through the green of the weeds.

Again Mitsuo lifted the hoe. But instead of chopping among the weeds, he dropped the hoe and knelt. Then he parted the grass and looked at where a spider had spun its web on the leaves of a milkweed. The night dew had caught on the threads, and each drop shone like a small sun.

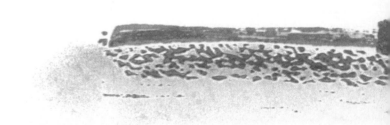

"Mitsuo!"

"I am cutting weeds," Mitsuo called
as he raised the hoe and let it fall.

"One milkweed cannot matter,"
Mitsuo said to himself. "And I
would like to see a hundred suns
every morning."

Carefully he cut other plants away
until the milkweed stood alone,
its web shining with its many suns.

"Mitsuo!"

"I have begun, Father." And the hoe
rose and fell, rose and fell.

"Cr-r-r-oak!"

Mitsuo stopped and listened.
He heard nothing except the sounds
of morning. He raised the hoe.

"Cr-r-r-oak!"

"Again I have heard a frog,"
said Mitsuo. "How can that be?
A pond is not here. Where the willow
dips its leaves is where the frogs
should sing."

"Cr-r-r-oak!"

Mitsuo again raised his hoe.
He did not raise it to chop weeds.
He held it just high enough to part
the weeds so that he could see
what was hidden beneath them.

There was a puddle of water, but it was not big enough for a big frog. It was just big enough for a frog until it grew pond large.

"There must be a frog," said Mitsuo, "for did I not hear its song? Why is there no frog to be seen?"

"Cr-r-r-oak!"

Mitsuo looked as hard as he could. Then he saw the frog. Its big eyes were shining up at Mitsuo.

"Cr-r-r-oak!"

"Frog, sir," said Mitsuo, "you are in the Yamada vegetable garden. If you stay in your water, from where will come the Yamada vegetables when summer is here?"

"Cr-r-r-oak!" said the frog.

"Of course," Mitsuo said, "if I
did not eat carrots every Tuesday,
we would not need to plant so many.
Then you could stay in your own pond."

"Cr-r-r-oak!" said the frog.

"I will do this," said Mitsuo. He
pulled the hoe back and let the weeds
close over the frog's home.

Then Mitsuo worked hard to cut away
the weeds. But he left enough of them
to hide the puddle where the frog lived.

Mitsuo leaned on his hoe. "How fine it looks," he said. "It is like a marsh where the best frogs are to be found."

"Cr-r-r-oak!" said the frog.

Wo-Nee Materials Center

16

"Mitsuo!"

"I am working, Father." Mitsuo's hoe went up and down, up and . . .

Mitsuo stopped again. He looked at the blue and yellow and orange and violet flowers. It didn't matter that they were flowering weeds. They were flowers to Mitsuo. And over the flowers there was the humming sound of bees.

"Mitsuo! Mitsuo!" his father called. Mitsuo did not answer.

"Mitsuo!"

"I am doing what I should do, Father." But Mitsuo's hoe did not cut into the field of flowers.

"I cannot cut the flowers now," Mitsuo said to himself. "The bees must have nectar to make their honey. It would not be good for the Yamadas to go without honey this winter. Would it not be better to leave the flowers for the bees? But if I leave the flowers, will there be enough land left for the vegetables?"

Mitsuo looked at the garden. "There will be enough," he said. "Anyway, I can always give up spinach on Wednesday."

"Mitsuo!"

"I am working, Father!" And he was.
Mitsuo pretended that he was a machine.
He cut his way through the weeds,
leaving rows of brown earth.

But what machine could stop and see
what Mitsuo saw? Could a machine see
the butterfly that had just come
from its chrysalis? Could a machine
watch the butterfly unfold its wings
to the drying warmth of the sun?

Never had a boy been as careful
as Mitsuo Yamada. His hoe tiptoed
about the plant. Not even the loudness
of a shadow fell across the butterfly.

The butterfly moved its wings
to the feel of the air, but it did not
notice Mitsuo.

When Mitsuo saw how many weeds he
had left, he shook his head and said
to himself, "It is much too much.
I will have to cut down more weeds.
The butterfly will fly away,
but there will be other butterflies."

Just then sunlight showed each
color of the butterfly's wings.

"No." Mitsuo shook his head.
"There will be many butterflies,
but there never will be another one
like this. I will work twice as fast
and twice as hard as before. Then it
will not matter how many weeds I
have left."

And he did work twice as fast and
twice as hard. He was working so fast
that he might not have seen the nest
in the grass, if he hadn't been a boy.

It was the smallest of nests,
and in it was a tiny speckled bird.
The bird did not fly off but feathered
large against its fear of Mitsuo.

"I will not hurt your eggs. You are the bravest of birds. From the eggs in your nest will hatch eagles."

"Tweet," said the bird.

"No, no, little bird," said Mitsuo, "they will not be real eagles. Like you they will be small speckled birds. And that it can be so, I, Mitsuo Yamada, will not break apart your nest."

"Tweet," said the bird.

"Mitsuo!"

"I am working, Father."

The bird's bright eyes followed Mitsuo as he chopped around and around its nest. The weeds fell under his hoe until a band of cleared ground lay between the bird and Mitsuo.

When the bird saw that Mitsuo did
not mean to harm it, it flew about
Mitsuo's head as if to thank him.
Then it returned to the four blue eggs
lying in its nest.

"That is right," said Mitsuo.
"To receive without thanks is not
to be worthy of favors." Mitsuo bowed
to the bird.

"Mitsuo!"

Mitsuo lifted his hoe. "I am
working, Father."

"Come, it is time to eat."

Mitsuo was always ready to eat.
He put the hoe over his shoulder
and started to leave the field.
But before he left, he turned once
to look at all that he had done.

There was the milkweed where the
web had caught a hundred suns.
There the land was cleared, except
where the frog had made a pond
of its own from a rain puddle.
There in the middle of the cleared
earth some flowers grew, busy with bees.
And there was the butterfly.
Mitsuo would remember its wings in the
sunlight long after it had flown away.

"Tweet," said the bird as it flew
around Mitsuo.

Mitsuo nodded his head. "It was a
good morning's work," he said,
"a good morning's work, indeed!"